THE
WHALE WHO SAVED
US

NICOLA DAVIES

with illustrations by
ANNABEL WRIGHT

**WALKER
BOOKS**

Chapter One

It was cold for spring. The sort of day when fingers get frostbite fast if they aren't covered up. Suki stomped down the street, her hands pushed into her pockets, staring miserably down at the dirty snow. It had been a bad day: she'd been suspended from school for hitting Paul Kasugak in Mrs Napier's class, because he'd said horrible things about her big brother Levi. Levi and his best friend

Peter were always in trouble and now they'd run off. No one had seen either of them for a week.

"Come to a bad end, I bet," Paul had said. "Frozen solid under a snowdrift."

That was when Suki had hit him. Everyone knew how many young Inuit came to a bad end committing crimes or driven to take their own lives because there were no jobs and there was no hope. But not *her* brother, not Levi.

Suki shivered inside her down jacket and tried to shake the thought of losing Levi from her mind. Doughnuts, that was what she needed to cheer her up! She stopped at the coffee shop and bought three, one of each of her favourite flavours. They would freeze if she didn't hurry home, so she quickened her pace: past the video shop; past the bar where Levi and Peter hung out; across the street and up the stairs to their apartment above the dentist's surgery.

A light was showing through a window. Suki's heart leapt; had Levi come home? She stamped the snow off her boots and burst into the hallway. But there was no Levi, only her mother, Sarah, standing with two suitcases at her feet. Her face was tense, her lips pursed tight as if trying to hold something inside. Her words hardly seemed able to squeeze their way out.

"Your brother's in Redknife," she said. "Peter too."

Suki felt a surge of relief; at least that meant Levi wasn't "frozen solid under a snowdrift". But Redknife was 500 miles away!

"What are they doing *there*?" Suki exclaimed.

Sarah wouldn't meet her daughter's eyes. "The less you know the better," she said. "Now pick up this case. We're going to the airport. I gotta go to Redknife and I'm sending you to Whale Bay, to stay with Great-Granny Jaiku."

Suki's mouth opened like a fish. *"Why?"*

"Because I can't be in Redknife *and* here to watch out for you," Sarah snapped. "Now pick up this case!" Sarah was stony with determination.

Suki picked up the suitcase, and backed out of the door, but she wasn't ready to give in. Wherever

Levi was, that was where she wanted to be too. She took a deep breath and tried to sound calm not angry. "Why can't I come to Redknife?" she asked.

Sarah wasn't going to budge. "Because I don't want you mixed up in Levi's trouble," she said. "You're going to Jaiku's and that's the end of it."

"But Great-Granny Jaiku hasn't seen me since I was little," Suki protested.

"So that's a good reason to visit now!" said her mum, shutting the door behind them.

Suki stood at the top of the steps while Sarah bumped her suitcase down to the street.

"But I'll miss school!" she wailed, using one last argument that *might* work, but Sarah only raised an eyebrow and said, "Huh! You think I don't know you've been suspended again?"

The taxi pulled up and Sarah got in.

"Come *on*, Suki!"

They were almost at the airport before either of them spoke again. Sarah gave a deep sigh.

"What is the matter with you kids today?" she said quietly to the taxi window.

Suki didn't speak, but she knew the answer. They were stuck between two worlds, the old one where Inuit had hunted seals and lived in snow houses and the new one of cities and computers. Stuck, without feeling they belonged in either. And now, to make everything worse, she was being sent away from her brother, to some old relative she hadn't seen in years, in a place where there wasn't even a coffee shop! Sometimes she hated her mum.

They didn't speak at the airport either, but when it was time to say goodbye there were tears in Sarah's eyes. Suki climbed the metal stairway to get onto the little plane, her own eyes threatening to spill over. She plonked herself into a window seat. Then she remembered this was only the second time she'd been on a plane, and felt a tiny beat of excitement. But it was stupid to feel excited about a plane ride when anything could be happening to Levi.

Besides, it would probably be too cloudy to see a thing. Suki bit her lip and felt her emotions rolling around in her chest like washing in a drier.

There were very few passengers. Suki had two seats all to herself. Almost as soon as she'd done up her seatbelt, the propellers whizzed to a blur and the plane raced down the runway. It took off with a lurch, and Suki pressed her nose to the little window by her seat. It wasn't cloudy after all! The sky was completely clear. Ice crystals sparkled in the air like spilt glitter as the plane rose through the slanting sunlight. Already Ullavit was shrinking. Up here in the far, far North, everyone called it "the City", but in the South it would be no more than a small town. The plane rose, and the houses and shops shrank to the size of sugar-cubes, then match heads and then just pinpricks, tiny fleas on the giant silvery-dark pelt of frozen land and sea. The sinking sun threw shadows eastwards from the mountains and streaked the sea ice with pink light. Down there, in her ordinary life in the busy state capital, the Arctic was just something she planned to escape from as soon as she was old enough. She had never thought about *this*, the huge, cold wilderness in which she lived. Now, vast and beautiful, it took her breath away. For the whole journey she gazed through the window and forgot all about Levi and Great-Granny Jaiku, and even about the three doughnuts, uneaten in her bag.

But as the plane came in to land at Whale Bay, Suki's heart sank again. The place looked like a selection of small parcels, dropped on the sea's edge and left for the snow to cover. A few dots of yellow light showed in the twilight, but that was all. It was clear that nothing ever happened here. Suki was sure she'd be the only passenger who would get off; the others would be going to the bigger settlements along the coast, where men from the South were prospecting for oil in the sea and gold in the mountains. She was surprised when four *qallunaaq** men got off too. They all wore expensive down jackets, each with the same logo on the sleeve,

---

*qallunaaq the word for white people in Inuktitut, the language spoken in Nunavut Province in northern Canada.

a green circle around a red hand. They carried huge holdalls from which the legs of tripods and other strange equipment poked, and strode ahead of her, talking. Suki struggled through the doors of the tiny terminal building after them and looked around. The men had already passed through the exit doors, and were climbing into a black four-by-four with the red hand symbol on its doors. Would there be anyone to meet *her*? she wondered. She checked her phone, but of course there was no signal here! Suddenly Suki felt very, very small and alone.

Then a slight Inuk* man in a dirty blue parka came hurrying through the doors. His face, framed by the fur around his hood, was a landscape of wrinkles from which his eyes glinted, bright as a bird's.

"Suki? Sarah's girl?" he said.

Suki nodded. Then the man spoke to her in Inuktitut, and for a moment Suki's mind froze. She and her mum always spoke English at home because that's what her dad spoke. It was a while since she'd

---

*Inuk the native people of the Arctic are known as Inuit. One Inuit person is called an Inuk.

spoken her native language outside a classroom. The man looked worried. He repeated what he'd said and, from somewhere that felt deeper than just her brain, the words came.

"*Qanuinngittunga!*" she answered him. *I'm fine!*

"Ah! You understand!" The old man beamed. "Thank goodness, because my English is not so good these days." He pushed his cap back on his head with a hand as knobbly as a piece of drift-wood.

"I guess you don't remember me," he went on, "I'm your Great-Uncle Noah. Last time I saw you, you were about the size of a rabbit."

"You're Granny Jaiku's brother, right?" Suki said.

Uncle Noah nodded. "*Baby* brother. Though not so baby now, eh?" he chuckled.

He reached to take her suitcase. Suki wasn't sure someone so old could manage a heavy case, but he lifted it onto his shoulder as if it weighed no more than a bag of flour.

"I'd have been here sooner, but I was fishing,"

he said, "and then that Red Hand Oil Company car almost ran me off the road! As if it's not enough that they scare every seal and whale in the bay with their noise and nonsense."

His wrinkles scrunched up into the fiercest frown Suki had ever seen, and just as quickly smoothed into a smile.

"Listen to me going on!" he laughed. "I expect you just want your supper, eh? Come on, let's get out of here!"

Outside, a fluorescent lamp flickered down onto the ice. Suki looked around for Noah's car but could only see an ancient snowmobile. It had a small trailer hooked on the back, into which Noah put her case. Then he climbed nimbly astride the machine and started her up.

"Hop on behind and hold tight!" he told her.

Suki pulled her scarf over her nose, tightened the hood of her parka and got up behind him. She'd been on a snowmobile before with Levi. He'd driven so fast he'd made her scream and then fall off. But

Noah was a more careful driver, and although the ride was over bumpy snow Suki felt quite safe.

The village lay below them making a curve around the ice-filled bay, with mountains on either side, like protecting arms. The snowmobile shooshed down the snaking track towards it. Noah switched off the headlights. There was no need for them. The sky was filled with a pearly gleam

that reflected on the snow and ice. There would be no real night this far north until the end of the summer*. Suki could hear the quiet, even over the buzz of the snowmobile: no sirens, or shouting voices, or trucks, like there were back home. Just the big, silent Arctic twilight.

The cold was deeper here. Suki could feel its icy fingers reaching under her clothes. She hoped they would be at Granny Jaiku's soon, but just as they were getting close to the houses, Noah changed direction and left the edge of the village behind. For a moment Suki thought they were heading out into the middle of nowhere, then she spotted a bungalow and a barn tucked behind a little bump of a hill, halfway across the bay.

By the time they got there, Suki was cold to the bone. She stood shivering, while Noah put the snowmobile into the barn. Somewhere, on the other side of the house, dogs were barking.

"No one else in Whale Bay has sled dogs any more," Noah told her sadly, as he came out of the

*Inside the Arctic Circle spring nights are short and from May to September there is twenty-four-hour daylight.

barn. "It's a struggle to keep them fed. But I couldn't live without mine."

Suki tried to smile but she was too cold.

"Come," Noah said, "let's get you inside!" He carried her case to the door and set it down.

The bungalow door opened, spilling yellow light onto the snow like treacle, and an old lady stood in the doorway.

"Welcome, Sarah's child!" said Great-Granny Jaiku. "Welcome!"

Chapter Two

Noah went out to settle his dogs and left Suki standing awkwardly by her suitcase. The lounge and kitchen were one not very big room. There was no TV as far as Suki could make out, only a radio.

"May I phone Mum, and let her know I got here safe?" Suki asked politely.

"We'll call her from Cousin Eli's tomorrow morning," Granny Jaiku said, without turning her attention from the pots on the stove. "We don't have a phone out here." She spoke as if having a phone was some sort of exotic luxury. Suki stared at her great-granny's back in disbelief, and felt a very, very long way from home.

"Here," said Granny Jaiku, "this'll warm you up!" The old lady handed Suki a big mug of hot chocolate. "I know you don't remember me much," she said, "but I remember you. When you'd just learned to walk. Look, there you are!"

She pointed to the wall beside the stove, where there was a photo of a small girl cuddling a big dog.

"That's you!" Jaiku said. "You loved that dog of Noah's."

Suki looked at the picture and a memory rose up inside her of the dog's soft fur and the warmth of her great-granny's smile. Jaiku pointed to another photo.

"This one is your mum," she said. "She was such a happy child."

Suki looked at the little girl's wide smile. It was hard to imagine that her mum had *ever* smiled like that. "Who's the lady in the picture with her?" Suki asked.

"Ah," said Jaiku, stroking the image of the young woman with her finger. "That's my Evie – your grandma who died."

Suki knew that her mother had been an orphan at five years old, but for the first time it seemed real: there was little Sarah, so small, and her mum, Evie, pretty and still a teenager. Suki felt a sudden pang of regret that she had parted from her mother today without a kind word.

Jaiku sighed and sat down at the table opposite Suki. "You know me and Noah raised Sarah, here, after Evie died?"

Suki nodded. Her mum had told her that much at least, but nothing more. Suki looked down at her chocolate. "Mum doesn't really talk much about when she was little."

"Well," Jaiku said, "she liked being sent away to high school in the city more than she liked being here." The old lady sighed. "We've had our differences but she's still my granddaughter and she'll always be welcome here, same as you."

"Thanks, Granny Jaiku!" Suki said.

Jaiku rose and began to clatter the pots on the stove again. Suki watched her great-granny bustling about, preparing the meal. Jaiku was small and slight, like Sarah, not at all Suki's tall, solid build. But although she must be almost eighty years old, she moved with the energy of a young woman.

"I've made proper Inuit food to build you up!" she said. "As soon as Noah stops talking to his dogs, we'll eat."

The door opened and Noah came in with a blast of frosty air. "Woah! It's a cold one out there all right," he said. "What I need is some food to warm my belly!"

Her mum usually bought pizza or packs of burgers from the supermarket, so Suki had never had seal stew before. It tasted weird. Like rust and seaweed. But she didn't want to hurt Jaiku's feelings, or be disrespectful to an old person, so she chewed carefully and tried to smile when she swallowed.

"Where did you get the seal meat?" Suki asked politely.

Noah laughed. "Out there," he said, "on the ice. I shot three last week. It's the Inuit way to share so we gave most of the meat to the community, of course, but we kept some!"

Suki couldn't keep the astonishment out of her voice. "You're a hunter?"

Noah laughed. "You figured I was too old, eh?"

Suki blushed.

"No, not yet! Besides, we got to hunt – store-bought food is too expensive. Most of Whale Bay eats what I catch," Noah said. "Folks prefer to watch TV instead of going hunting."

"Not me," said Jaiku. "Father taught me to catch fish and shoot seals long before you were born, *little* brother! There's a long tradition of women hunting in this family."

Noah grinned at Suki. "Oh, now she's going to tell you a story!" he said. "I'm going to check on the dogs."

"Again?" Jaiku scolded. "It's a good thing you don't have a wife, the time you spend with those animals!"

"It's *why* I don't have a wife, sister, so that I *can*!"

Jaiku shook her head and laughed as he shrugged on his parka and slipped through the door. Then she turned to Suki. "Come," she said. "I'll show you something."

The old lady led Suki into a tiny bedroom which was just long enough for a narrow bed. Instead of a bedside table, there was a battered old chest, like something out of a pirate movie. Jaiku sat on the bed and patted the place beside her. "This will be your room," she said. "Come. Sit."

Suki did as she was asked. Jaiku leant forward and opened the domed lid of the chest and pulled a small cloth bag from its dark depths. Inside was a piece of yellowed ivory.

"Walrus tusk," Jaiku said. "Look!"

Suki had seen carvings like this before – pictures scratched onto bits of animal bone or tooth, and stained black. It was called scrimshaw; the dad of a school friend did it for the tourists to buy. But this was different – someone had taken real trouble over it. The scratched lines were tiny, and the picture they created was detailed and delicate. It showed a whale, its dark back breaking the surface of a mirror-calm sea, and its breath like mist on the air. Beside it was an animal-skin boat, an

umiak, with six Inuit men paddling hard. Their faces were thin and gaunt and they looked worried. At the front of the boat, standing graceful as a dancer, was a young woman, her dark hair blowing in the wind. She was tall and strong and held a harpoon above her shoulder, ready to strike the whale!

Jaiku pointed to the woman. "This is our ancestor. My great-great-*great*-grandmother, Manattiaq!" she said, proudly.

"But I thought only men were allowed to hunt whales," Suki said.

"Usually." Jaiku smiled broadly. "But Manattiaq, she was very special, very famous among our people. She killed this whale and brought it ashore, just down the beach from here. She saved the whole village from starvation. They named her Whale Warrior!"

Suki's eyes grew wide: her ancestor sounded like some kind of superhero! Maybe life in Whale Bay hadn't *always* been dull.

"This is your family history. Evie was never interested, neither was your mum. But I think you're different. Like Manattiaq was different."

The way Jaiku said "different" it sounded like something good, something special. Suki felt that no one had ever said anything as nice about her before.

"Thanks, Granny Jaiku!" she said. Jaiku laid her small hand on Suki's arm for a moment, light and warm.

"No need to thank me, child!" she said, getting up. "Now, it's bedtime! You look tired."

Jaiku turned at the door and Suki looked up at her. "Granny Jaiku," she asked, "did Mum tell you what sort of trouble Levi was in?"

Jaiku shook her head and sighed. "Not yet," she said. "But he's always gone his own way."

"He's a good person really, Granny," Suki said. "Just kind of wild."

Jaiku smiled sadly. "He is your *anikuluk**, as Noah is mine!"

Suki nodded.

"Try not to worry about Levi," Jaiku said. "Who knows, you're smart – maybe you'll find a way to help him."

*anikuluk word for a brother that a woman is especially fond of.

Chapter Three

Suki opened her eyes. It was *very* early, but the room was bright with sunlight and somebody's dogs were barking. Where was she? Ah yes, Granny Jaiku's house. She lay still, remembering the reason she was here: something bad had happened to Levi. Suki found her throat grow tight with held-in tears.

Well, at least she had something to comfort herself with. Without getting up, she reached into her school backpack, pulled out the paper bag of doughnuts and peered inside; orange, cinnamon or chocolate, first?

"Suki? Breakfast!" Jaiku was calling from the kitchen. No time for all three then. Chocolate now, orange and cinnamom later.

She was about to take the first delicious bite when Noah's words came back to her:

It's the Inuit way to share.

She put the chocolate doughnut back in the bag.

"Coming, Granny Jaiku," she called. "Coming!"

Suki ate the bannock* that Jaiku had made. It was plain, but hot and good, made fresh in Granny's old skillet. The radio crackled away with the morning news from the state capital, while Noah and Jaiku discussed their choice of doughnut. Suddenly the newscaster's voice silenced them:

"RCMP* officers were called to a house in downtown Ullavit yesterday afternoon, where eighteen-year-old Peter Oolik, son of Finance Minister David Oolik, and nineteen-year-old Levi Kaluak were found unconscious. Both boys have been flown to hospital in Redknife for specialist attention and remain in a critical condition. Community spokesman Elliot Nakasuk said, 'Like many of our young people, these two young men have struggled to find a reason to live. We must be grateful that they were found before their attempt at suicide could succeed.'"

That was why Levi and Peter were in Redknife! Suki stared at Jaiku and Noah in shock.

"Mum *knew* when she put me on the plane!" she cried as Jaiku flicked off the radio.

---

*bannock bread cooked in a pan, either on the stove or over an open fire. A tradition adopted from Scottish whalers.

*RCMP Royal Canadian Mounted Police – the police force in Canada.

"She was trying to protect you, Suki!" Jaiku said. "Don't be angry with her."

"Those darned reporters would be all over you in Ullavit!" Noah added. "What with that boy being the minister's son and all."

Suki took a breath; she felt like she was drowning. "Is Levi going to die?"

Jaiku looked grim but determined. "No!" she said firmly. "No, he's not!"

Noah said, "He'll be getting the best treatment at that big hospital in Redknife."

Suki took a huge gasping breath. "I want to go to him!"

Jaiku shook her head. "You can't go flying off to Redknife. It's a lot of money for a ticket."

"Besides," Noah added before Suki opened her mouth to protest, "there are no flights out today. "

"I'll go to Eli's this morning, and call your mum," Jaiku said. "See what more I can find out."

"And you and I, Suki," said Noah, "we're going to catch some fish."

Suki shook her head. "No! I want to go with Granny Jaiku!" she cried.

"You can't!" said Noah quietly. "I need your help, and if we don't catch any fish all we'll have to eat is your doughnuts."

Suki looked to her grandmother, hoping for support, but Jaiku only shrugged and said, "That's the way it is up here."

Suki leapt up, ready to argue, but she saw that Jaiku and Noah weren't angry. They were just telling her the way things were.

Suki's cloth parka wasn't warm enough for a day on the ice, so Noah fetched her one that Jaiku had made for Sarah.

"It's made from caribou* skin and the hood is Arctic hare."

It was a bit grubby, but still supple, and the fur-lined hood was silky soft. It was a little too big but more comfortable than Suki expected.

"Take these too," Noah said, emerging from a

*caribou Canadian reindeer.

dark back room – "Sealskin kamiiks*. Jaiku made these too. She makes the best boots in the whole Arctic!"

The boots had a lining of the softest leather, and a pattern of dark and light triangles sewn into the outside. The stitches were tiny and neat, like little teeth holding the different parts of the boots together.

"They're stitched with sinew*," Noah told her. "It swells when it's wet and keeps the water out of the needle holes."

Suki put them on and stepped around the kitchen. They were so light and warm it felt like walking on a cloud. The pleasure of it made her smile in spite of the news about Levi.

"You won't slip in those and you won't get cold or wet," Noah told her. "Good boots can save a hunter's life. Now, let's hitch up the dogs!"

"Aren't we going on the snowmobile?"

"No. Jaiku's taking it," Noah said. "In any case, dogs are much better than any machine!"

*kamiiks boots made of animal skin, caribou or seal.
*sinew tough string-like parts of animal bodies that join muscles to bones.

Suki wasn't sure what to be most surprised at: that her eighty-something great-granny could drive a snowmobile, or that she was about to get a ride on a dog sled.

The dogs were tethered in the yard behind the barn, lying in the snow with their furry tails curled over their noses, but when they saw Noah, they leapt to their feet and began to bark.

"I've loaded the sled," Noah said. "All we need to do is harness the dogs."

Each dog had a harness that fitted over its head and round its body. Noah showed Suki how to put them on. In spite of their size and energy the big sled dogs were gentle and friendly. They had bright, intelligent eyes and six out of the eight of them seemed to know exactly how to get into a harness. They lifted their feet up, like her mum threading her arms into her coat when Suki held it up for her. The other two wriggled and wagged, and had to be coaxed. Noah laughed.

"These are youngsters – they're still learning what to do."

Next, Noah clipped the dogs onto the traces that would pull the sled. His face grew serious as he did this and he spoke quietly to the dogs, attaching them two by two.

"You have to be careful who you pair with who," he explained. "If I put Shadow – the big black one – with Blue, they fight. But if I put Shadow with Moss

in front, then Blue and Rumble pull harder to keep up."

By the time all the dogs were harnessed, they were so excited that it was impossible to hear anything above their barks and yelps. Suki climbed on the sled, and sat down on the caribou hide that covered the load, while Noah stood at the back. He called out, making a sound that wasn't quite a word but that had a clear, hopeful ring to it.

"U-uk! U-uk!"

The dogs knew at once what it meant! They were off, racing over the snow at a speed that felt much faster than a car. There was no more barking and yelping now, only the sighing of the runners and the pattering of paws. Suki's heart leapt. Perhaps being at Jaiku's house wasn't so boring after all.

The sun was already high in the sky. At this time of year it climbed further every day. A month ago there had been just nine hours of daylight, now there were almost fifteen. Suki scrunched up her eyes against the light. In front, the frozen sea stretched to the horizon. Behind them, the little arc of houses looked out to the bay where four snow-mobiles with laden trailers whined.

"Red Hand Oil men," Noah said with a scowl. "Surveying. They're gonna build a dock in the bay, big enough for oil tankers."

Her uncle wore his fierce frown again.

"That will be good, won't it?" said Suki.

"Not for us. Noise and pollution are no good for hunting and fishing."

"Then can't you fight it?"

Noah sighed. "The fight's gone out of the people in Whale Bay. Most of the elders sit on their sofas and watch TV all day." He shook his head and looked sad. "But today," he said, his smile return-ing, "we're fishing!"

He urged his dog team on again. "*U-uk! U-uk!*"

The dogs pushed their noses forward, as if they could not wait to find out what lay in front of them. Suki felt the same, the world of white and blue seemed all new, just hers, to be discovered!

For a moment she was completely happy, until she remembered Levi.

She turned to Noah. "I wish Levi was here," she said. "I think he'd love this!"

Noah leant forward and patted her shoulder. "You can tell him about it – when he's better," he said. "Telling is another kind of sharing."

Suki nodded. She *would* tell Levi; he *would* get better! And she would have more to share if she thought about the dogs, and the sled and the sunlight, and not about Levi, lying in a hospital bed.

Chapter Four

They slowed down near a spot that Noah said was good for fishing. It didn't look different from any other spot to Suki, but then Noah pointed out the cleft in the hill behind them that showed they were above the place where the frozen river ran into the bay.

"I made a couple of fishing holes yesterday, and I set a net between 'em, but we'll need to break the fresh ice."

Suki looked to where Noah pointed and saw two mounds of snow about a basketball court apart.

Noah brought the sled to a stop close to the first mound. Suki jumped down and the dogs flopped in the snow.

"Let's see what I caught!" Noah said.

The mounds were made of the snow that had been scraped off two circles of ice, each about the size of Jaiku's kitchen table. In the centre of the circles, a hole had been hacked into the thick ice; the

net had been strung under the ice between the two holes, held up by a rope tied to a wooden stake at each end. Noah told Suki to stand at one hole, break the ice that had formed overnight around the end of the net, and then to untie the rope and pull it tight. Her sealskin boots stopped her slipping as she did as Noah asked.

"Now, let the rope out slowly," Noah called. "If the net sinks, it'll be too hard to pull it up from the bottom!"

Suki wrapped her mittened hands around the rope and held on, letting it out as Noah pulled the net up through the other hole. At last, when there were just a few feet left sticking out of the ice hole,

Noah yelled for her to let go. She raced towards him
to see if they had caught anything.

Thirty big fish lay at Noah's feet, some of them
still alive and flapping about. Noah hit the live ones
on the head to kill them and began to clean them
with his knife, leaving the guts in a pile.

"That's the share for the foxes, maybe a snack
for a bear too!" Noah said, then he sliced a small
fillet from one of the fish and offered it to Suki.
"Eat!" he said. "It's good!"

She didn't want to be rude so she took the scrap of raw fish and put it in her mouth. It was cold and slippery.

"Chew!" Noah told her. "You got to taste it."

He laughed at the face she made. "We used to eat a lot of things raw in the old days," he said. "Only seal-blubber lamps to cook on when I was little!"

Suki swallowed the cold fish and tried to look cheerful.

Noah showed her how to gut and cut the fish so it could be carried home to be smoked or dried. He praised the neatness of Suki's fillets and how fast she learned.

"My teachers say I'm a slow learner," Suki said. "I'm always in trouble."

"They'd change their minds if they saw you today!" Noah grinned.

While Suki worked, Noah gathered in the net and stowed it in the trailer. Then he got out a little camping stove and cooked a fish for them. Suki perched on the sled and ate the hot, pink flesh and crispy skin. It was almost the best thing she'd ever eaten. Noah laughed at her again when he saw how she sucked every last bit from her fingers.

"Next time, you can try fresh seal! Or maybe narwhal *maktaaq**. That's so good!"

"You catch whales?"

"Well, yes!" Noah laughed at Suki's astonished face. "Narwhals are whales but quite little ones! They come along the ice edge in the spring and we go after 'em in kayaks and *umiaks*. But nowadays the ice often melts too early and some years we don't catch any."

"What about big whales?" Suki asked. "I'd like to see one of those!" She thought of Manattiaq holding her harpoon, her long hair blowing in the wind, but Noah shook his head.

"Like the bowhead you mean? We call it *Arviq**; it was the heart of our people at one time. A whole village would hunt a whale together. But the Yankee whalers killed almost all of them a hundred years ago. Nobody's caught a bowhead whale

---

***maktaaq** Inuktitut word for beluga or narwhal skin. It is rich in vitamins and minerals.
***arviq** Inuktitut word for bowhead whale.

in a long time," he said. "A few come sometimes in the summer but no one remembers how to hunt them..."

They repacked the sled and turned back over the ice, but Noah didn't head straight home along the coast. He steered inland, towards what looked like a pile of pebbles. As they got closer Suki saw the pebbles were boulders. Noah stopped the sled and pointed up the slope to where two slender grey poles stuck up out of the snow like fingers.

"Those are bowhead jawbones. They say they're from the whale that Manattiaq killed. The elders put the skull up there so the whale could still see the ocean. We always used to do that out of respect," he said. "When Jaiku and I were small, that was our family's summer camp. Those bones held up the tent, made of caribou skin."

"Can we go up and look?" Suki asked.

"You can take your young legs up there!" Noah laughed. "I'll wait with the dogs. But be quick. This air is changing and I don't like what it might bring."

The *crunch crunch* of the snow was the only sound as Suki dug her toes in and trudged up the slope. She reached the flat place where the camp had been. The jawbones stuck up like old, grey stone. Even half buried in snow, they were so huge that it was impossible to imagine that they were the bones of a creature, and not the rocky skeleton of the Earth itself.

Suki rested a mitten on one of the jawbones and imagined the vast animal of which it had once been a part. How would it feel to be close to one out on the ocean? She felt a thrill pass along her arm at the thought of it. No wonder Manattiaq was famous; killing a bowhead was like killing a magical giant – a wonderful but also a terrible feat: the great life of the whale had ended, but a whole village had been saved.

What was it like back then? she wondered. Before houses and cars, TVs and doughnuts, when all you had was what you could hunt or make? If you made a mistake or weren't skilful enough, you would freeze or starve. Maybe Levi would have been happy in a time like that; wildness might be a useful thing for a whale hunter.

Noah was waving at her. Shouting too by the look of him, but his voice was swallowed up in the space between them. The air was thickening with a silent, freezing fog that was rolling in from the ocean. Already the fishing holes had disappeared. Suki rushed down the slope, scrambling and tumbling to reach Noah before he disappeared.

The icy mist caught in Suki's chest.

"I called and called," Noah said. "You didn't come."

"I'm sorry."

"You need to pay attention when you're out here, Suki!" Noah scolded. "Nowadays the weather is hard to read. It changes faster than it used to. Get up on the sled. We need to go!"

They set off at once. Everything was turned to dense, milky whiteness. Only the dogs closest to the sled were visible, their heads down, pulling hard. But were they going the right way? It was impossible to tell! A pulse of fear went through Suki's belly. She turned to her uncle and said, "I'm sorry. It's my fault we're lost!"

Noah's frown dissolved into laughter. "We're not lost!"

"How do you know which way to go?" Suki cried.

"The *uqalurait* – snow tongues – tell you." Noah pointed to the snowy ground passing underneath the sled. Its surface was covered in little rounded waves of snow, all facing the same way!

"The wind mostly blows from the north-west. It blows the snow into those shapes, that point away from the wind, south-east, and that's where the village is!"

Suki felt that Noah had let her into a magical secret – that even in the heart of the frozen fog, the tongues of snow told them how to get home! All around, the fog washed and wafted as if they were floating in an eternal white bubble, going nowhere. But Suki was no longer afraid.

The dogs sniffed out the last bit of the route, turning a little to the right until they almost bumped into the side of the barn. The snowmobile was already safely stowed so Jaiku must be home with news of Levi. Suki leapt from the sled and rushed into the house.

Jaiku was standing in the kitchen with her outside clothes still on. She looked so tired and sad that for a moment Suki feared the worst, but Jaiku said,

"He's alive. But he's in a coma and so is the other boy."

Suki sank into a chair and listened while Jaiku told her all she had found out. Of course Sarah was not at home. She was staying in Redknife to be near Levi. Jaiku had called the hospital and spoken to her there.

"She said Peter's father, Minister Oolik, is being a big help," Jaiku said, "but there's nothing you can do and she says it's best you stay here."

"I want to see my brother!" Suki wailed.

"You can see him when he wakes up," Jaiku said firmly.

"But what if he *never* wakes up?" Suki cried.

Suki felt the tears spilling onto her cheeks. She ran into her bedroom and threw herself on her bed. Noah's voice carried from the kitchen, reassuring his sister: "For sure he'll come round. *For sure.*"

Jaiku answered sadly, "But he won't be really safe until he finds a reason to live!"

Chapter Five

They all fell silent when the news came on the next morning, but there was nothing about Minister Oolik's son and his friend, on either the radio station from Ullavit or the community radio from the next settlement up the coast. There was nothing the next morning, or the morning after that. Suki couldn't decide if that was bad or good.

"No news is good news," Jaiku said. "We'll try and call your mum at the hospital later."

Noah disappeared into his bedroom and came out with a package, which he put on the table.

"This was your mum's," he said. "It still works fine."

Suki opened the package. Inside was a little microphone and an ancient cassette player.

"You can record something for your brother," Noah explained, "and we can send it with the post. Eli was in hospital years ago and he said he could hear things when the doctors had put him to sleep, so maybe Levi can hear too."

Suki smiled. It was kind of Noah, but no one had used cassettes for years. She didn't want to hurt his feelings, so she said, "Thanks, Uncle Noah. I'll do something this morning."

"Ah," Noah replied, "no hurry, the post doesn't go until tomorrow. And I have something else for you to do this morning, as the weather is better. Sled training!"

The dogs barked and wagged their tails as Noah and Suki approached. Noah gave Suki four harnesses and told her to put them on Moss and Thunder, Blue and Walleye. They were the most experienced dogs and could almost have put their own harnesses on, so Suki was ready when Noah emerged from the barn pulling a small sled with smooth, curved runners.

"This is the one I use for training new dogs," he told her. "And people!"

Noah showed Suki where to put her feet and

how to balance on the end of the runners.

"It's your job to see what's coming and guide the dogs," he told her. "Their noses are good but your eyesight is better and you can see further than they can."

They hooked up the four dogs, then Noah sat on the little platform at the front of the sled.

"Let's go!" he said.

Suki tried to get the dogs going.

"U-uk!" she said.

"Louder!" Noah told her.

"Like you really mean it."

"U–UK!" Suki called

again; Thunder looked over his shoulder as if to say *"Is this kid really in charge?"* Then suddenly, with a jerk, the sled began to move. Suki almost fell off.

"Oh, I don't think I can do this!" she said.

"Yes, you *can*," Noah said firmly. "You need to pay attention with your mind and relax with your body. Think about what you're doing, not about anything else. As an Inuk, your life depends on that!"

Around and around the house and barn they went. First one way then another, making their circuits wider and wider as the mist lifted like a series of veils. Noah made her turn, and stop, again and again. She fell off four times and had to run to catch the sled. Noah didn't help at all; she had to do it all by herself. After a while he said, "Now let's see how fast you can get these dogs to run!"

Noah got off the sled and pointed towards the far side of the bay, where the arm of the mountain was just showing through the thinning fog.

"Go that way until you can cover the barn with your thumb, then come back."

"On my own?"

Noah nodded. Suki took a deep breath. "*U–UK*!" she said, and this time there was no hesitation, the dogs knew she was in charge. With only Suki's weight to haul, they made the sled fly over the snow. Faster and faster! Suki felt a knot in her tummy and felt her legs stiffen with fear. This was too fast, she couldn't do this on her own! Then the sled went over a bump she hadn't seen and she almost fell.

Pay attention, Noah's voice said in her head. Suki made herself stop thinking about being scared. She scanned ahead, over the dogs' wagging tails and hurrying feet. Sunlight was sifting through the mist like silver dust and the sled runners sang *shhh-hhhh shhhhhhhh*, like a breath. She breathed in time with it and glancing over her shoulder she saw that Jaiku's house was tiny, small enough almost for the end of her little finger to cover, let alone her thumb! She wheeled the dogs round and headed back.

A snowmobile had drawn up beside Noah, but it headed off towards the village as Suki brought the sled to a stop.

"You did well!" Noah said. Suki hid her face in her hood. She didn't want to show how pleased she was about having driven the team on her own.

"Who was that guy?" she asked.

"Pete Laplaque, a friend of our cousin's," Noah replied. "He's the other guy in the community who hunts. He says he saw narwhal at the ice edge under Fox Head. I'm going to run into the village and see if I can raise a narwhal crew. There's a few men I can drag off the couch!" He gave a wide grin. "You might get a taste of *maktaaq*. You go inside and tell Jaiku the plan."

Noah was very pleased when he got back from Whale Bay. Everything was arranged. They would set off as soon as possible and the rest of "the crew" would meet them under Fox Head with the boat.

"Our job is to set up camp for everybody."

A whirlwind of preparation followed, with Suki

ordered to fetch and carry by both her granny and her uncle. In an hour, the sled and the snowmobile trailer were loaded up and the mist had cleared to leave the sky clear blue. The snow and ice gleamed so that everyone had to wear snow goggles, or the brightness would blind them. Granny Jaiku, her small body covered in caribou and sealskin clothes, and her face mostly hidden by goggles, looked so much like an alien that Suki bit her cheeks so as not to giggle. She wished Levi could see his doughnut-loving little sister going off into the wilderness with two wrinkly old relatives covered in fur!

"Come on!" Noah called to her. "You can drive this dog team and Jaiku can ride in your sled."

They left the bay so far behind that the mountains were just a blur on the edge of the southern horizon.

"Not far now," Jaiku said, though how she could tell, Suki didn't understand. "We'll build an igloo," the old lady went on, "then the men will launch the *umiak* as soon as they've had some sleep."

Suki didn't say that she was afraid of sleeping without the walls of a real house around her. But she *did* like the idea of going in a boat to see narwhal!

"Can I go in the boat too, Granny Jaiku?"

"You'll have to show you can work hard first!"

Suki set her mouth in a determined line and, when they stopped, she didn't grumble once about being ordered around.

The dogs were tied up and given seal meat, then Noah and Jaiku each took a long, flat knife from the sled and began poking the snow, all around. At last they found a spot that satisfied them, and called Suki over.

"This is the right kind of snow for an igloo," said Noah.

"Yes," Jaiku agreed. "Not too hard so you can't cut it, not too soft so it won't hold a shape."

It looked like any other kind of snow to Suki.

"So I will cut the blocks..." Jaiku explained.

"I will shape and build..." Noah added. "And you,

Suki, with your good young back, will carry them."

For the next hour Suki carried big blocks of snow from where Jaiku cut them to a patch of slightly different snow a few metres away, where Noah used them to build the curved walls and domed roof of a snow house. Noah showed Suki how to shape the blocks to fit, angling them to make just the right curve so that the blocks would lean against each other and support the weight of the igloo. But she was kept so busy bustling between Jaiku and Noah

that she was too out of breath to really listen to what she was told.

The last block went into the top of the roof, trapping Noah inside, so the entrance to the igloo was made by Noah cutting his way out.

Jaiku set Suki to wriggling in and out with all the bedding, food and equipment while Noah and Jaiku stopped up any holes with loose snow. Inside the igloo it felt really cosy. Suki didn't feel afraid of sleeping there any more; in fact she rather thought she could lie down right then and sleep, but Jaiku was calling her.

"Come on, Suki, we've another igloo to build for the rest of the crew!"

How, Suki wondered, could she be more tired than her great-grandmother?

Chapter Six

Under the ice, directly below the place where Suki lay in the igloo, a huge whale was swimming. It sang as it swam, and the waterfall of high notes cascaded upwards into Suki's ears as she slept. Then it began to bang its great head against the ice, making the igloo shake, shake, shake...

"Come on, Suki, time to hunt narwhal!" Someone was shaking her shoulder hard, to pull her from her dreams. She opened her eyes to find Noah's face lit by his headlamp.

"Did the crew get here?" she yawned.

"You fell asleep before they arrived with the boat," Noah explained. "Now, it's time to go!"

"I dreamt there was a whale swimming under the igloo, Uncle Noah," Suki said sleepily, "banging its head on the ice."

"You did?" Noah smiled. "My grandpa used to say that when a whale passes under your boat you understand your place on Earth. Maybe it's the same for dream whales under the ice!" He grinned again and went outside.

Stars shone hazily in the blue twilight, snow-mobile headlights criss-crossed the camp and dogs barked. Noah introduced her to "the crew": Eli, a spry elder with twinkly eyes like Noah, one of Jaiku and Noah's many cousins; David Paniaq, a stern, sturdy man in his fifties, and his younger, less stern but more sturdy brothers, Zac and Joe, who all helped run the community store.

"I told them your dream," Noah said.

David nodded and his stern face broke into a smile. "I think it's a good sign!"

"Yes," Zac agreed. "Especially as you are Manattiaq's descendant!"

All the men except Joe seemed pleased that Suki was coming along. Joe didn't say anything.

"Don't worry about Joe," Jaiku whispered. "He's not used to the idea of girls on boats. No women in his family ever so much as hooked a fish!"

She smiled and handed Suki a pair of oilskin

trousers. "Here," she said, "these will keep you dry. Do whatever Noah or Eli tell you."

Suki nodded. "Aren't you coming, Granny Jaiku?"

"No, no. Me and Zac's wife, Lucy, will stay in camp with the dogs and make everything ready," she said. "The whale will like that." There wasn't time to ask what she meant. Suki climbed on the snowmobile behind Uncle Noah and they were off.

A ghost of green aurora was shimmering in the northern sky, but it soon faded as the sky began to brighten. The snow and ice glowed dull blue in the early light and the air was sharply cold. The snow-mobile thrummed along just quietly enough for Suki to be heard above it.

"What did Granny mean when she said the whale likes her to stay in camp?"

"That's what they told us when we were little," Noah said. "That the whale will only give itself if there is a comfortable home for it, with a lamp kept

i

burning. But that was for bowheads. I think maybe narwhal don't mind," Noah chuckled. "But Jaiku likes the old ways."

They stopped the snowmobiles close to the edge of the fast ice*, and dragged the boat to where patches of open water showed between lumps and chunks of frozen sea. The sea and air were completely still and the boat slipped into the water easily. David and Eli helped Suki aboard and showed her where to sit.

"In the prow here," David said. "I think you may have good whale-spotting eyes!"

"Keep your feet still in the bottom of the boat," Eli told her.

"Scraping boots make a big noise under the water and whales don't like it," Zac explained. Joe didn't say anything.

They used paddles to push the boat out to where there was a clear channel between the floes, then Noah started the outboard, at a gentle *put-put-put*. Light slanted over the horizon, sparkling on the water and illuminating every tiny splash. Noah

*fast ice the frozen sea that is anchored to the land.

stilled the engine and everyone looked and listened.

Pppffff, a tiny sound, like a mermaid kissing the surface! Instinctively Suki turned her head to it and saw a puff of breath, lit gold by the rising sun.

"There!" she breathed. *"There!"*

Pfffff another breath and then *pff pfffff pfff,* three more beside it. Tusks poked into the sunlight like spikes of twisted ice, and rounded heads showed at the surface. Then the curves of three black-and-white backs, with skin marbled like stone.

"Well done, Suki," said Eli.

Noah restarted the engine and they puttered gently towards the narwhal. As they grew nearer the men got ready. Eli had a rifle across his knees, David and Zac each held a harpoon with a rope attached to it. Suki's heart did backflips.

The narwhals dived; with an extra deep *pfff* of breath, their round blowholes shut. Their smooth backs bent into tight curves and their heart-shaped flukes* showed above the surface. Suki was struck by how neat their movements were and how perfectly quietly they went down. They were beautiful.

"There!" Zac cried. He stood up and threw his harpoon into the water on the other side of the boat. Fast as thinking Eli let off a shot and Joe another. Something grazed the underside of the boat; Suki felt it more than heard it. She glanced to her right and there, almost breaking the surface, was a narwhal! Its tusk

*flukes the broad tail of the whale, used to push it through the water. Each species has different-shaped flukes. Fluking up is another way to say that the whale is diving.

pierced the surface, far more robust than Suki had imagined, twisted all along its length. The shapes of two more narwhal were in the water below the first but all of them were gone so quickly she could only point wordlessly in the direction they had gone. Neither shots nor harpoon had found a mark and Suki couldn't decide if she was disappointed or relieved.

Zac reeled in his harpoon, Eli and Joe put the safety catches back on their guns and Noah turned the boat to follow after the narwhal. But the creatures were always just out of reach; after a while there was only sunlight, ice and sea. They puttered about amongst the floes, searching, as the sun rose higher and then stopped in a wide break of open water. David's stomach rumbled and then Zac's, and everyone, even Joe, smiled. Eider ducks splashed and made their *ooo ooo* calls on the sunlit water. A skein of geese passed over, flying west. Water slapped the bottom of the boat gently. Suki was in a dream with the stillness and calm all around them…

Then *hwwuuuufff!*

A sound so entirely unexpected that for a moment the whole crew froze. Less than twenty metres from where Suki sat in the prow of the little metal boat, a v-shaped head, as big as a pool table, broke the surface! It looked just like the picture on the scrimshaw tusk!

"*Arviq*?" Zac breathed in astonishment.

"*Arviq*!" Eli exclaimed. "Bowhead!"

The whale's back wallowed, black and shiny, so close beside them that their boat shivered with the wake it created.

Hwwwuuufff…

The whale breathed again, the twin slits of her blowholes clearly releasing a mist of warm breath into the cold air, from deep within the giant body. It rolled a little in the water, showing the curve of its mouth and the white patch of skin over its chin.

Hwuuuuuuffff. The whale took another breath, deeper still, echoing like the low note of a double bass.

"I haven't seen a bowhead for years!" said David.

"And never this early in the year," Noah added as Eli shook his head in amazed agreement.

But something had startled the whale. *Arviq* heard it before Suki and her companions, and the great body flexed with sudden alarm. The loud growling of a big outboard motor reached the humans' ears as the whale scooped under the surface, leaving a puff of poo in the water to show how scared it was. Looking out to sea, Suki saw a big, black motorboat with a red hand on the side weaving noisily through the mosaic of ice and ocean. The bowhead passed right under their boat, close enough for them to see how huge it was. Its tail beat in deep sweeps, heading for the edge of the fast ice. In less than a second, it was gone.

They waited with their engine off for the Red Hand survey boat to leave, but it just kept going back and forth, filling the air and water with its noise. The men exchanged dark looks.

"Narwhals aren't gonna come back with all

that racket!" Zac grumbled.

"It's scared every living thing for miles," David agreed.

Joe looked even more grumpy than ever, but the two older men, Noah and Eli, just sighed.

"Duck shooting?" Noah suggested with a hopeful smile.

"Guess so!" said Eli and the others nodded. Just then, the CB radio in Zac's jacket crackled to life. It was Lucy. The ice underneath the igloos was breaking up! Lucy and Jaiku were loading as much of the gear onto the dog sled as possible and heading towards the land, but with the sled fully loaded they would have to walk. The men exchanged worried looks.

"First we get a bowhead four months early, and then the fast ice splits way sooner than before!" exclaimed Zac.

"Must be that climate change everyone talks about," said Eli.

"Well, whatever it is," Noah said calmly, "we'd

better get back there. If the ice around the igloos is cracking, then the ice under the snowmobiles might not be safe."

Joe looked hard at Suki and spoke at last:

"Looks like your dream came true!" he said, as if the failure of the hunting expedition were somehow all her fault.

Chapter Seven

The snowmobiles were unharmed. Hurriedly they took the boat out of the water and began to make their way back to the igloos, but the journey that had taken just an hour in the morning now took almost three. The route was blocked by new leads*, and pressure ridges*. Time and again, they had to unload gear to lighten the vehicles enough to get them through the icy obstacle course. Every pair of hands was needed. Suki worked as hard as everyone else. What would her mum say if she could see her daughter now? Suki wondered, as she strained all her muscles to free a snowmobile runner from a crack. The girl who never finished an assignment at school and always wriggled out of her chores at home.

At last, they passed the igloos, now separated from each other by a huge crack, and caught up with Jaiku and Lucy. Joe turned to Suki. "You did well today. Worked like a boy!" he said.

*lead a long crack in the sea ice, "leading" from open water.
*pressure ridge when ice has been squashed by movements of the sea, or next door sheets of ice, it folds and buckles forming bumps and ridges.

Noah too praised her hard work. "You've grown a whole year in a day!" he told her.

Suki hid her face in her parka and smiled on the inside.

Jaiku was cheerful, but clearly very tired. She was limping too. She had fallen, Lucy quietly told Noah, when the ice had suddenly opened up between the igloos. Wearily, they reloaded the sleds and trailers. Jaiku was wrapped like a parcel and went in the dog sled that Noah was driving, and Suki got in Eli's snowmobile trailer.

On the way home the adults' talk was quiet and sad: a lot of expensive fuel had been used for nothing; there would be no *maktaaq* nor even any duck meat to eat. Everyone was cross about the disturbance the Red Hand boat had caused and worried by the early break-up of the ice. Would climate change bring a time when there would be no ice?

But in spite of their gloom, Suki was happy. She replayed the encounter with the bowhead whale over and over in her head, reliving every detail of it.

The experience glowed inside her and she imagined herself standing at the front of Eli's boat, with a harpoon above her head like Manattiaq.

Back at the house, Suki helped Jaiku inside and went straight back out to help Noah, then all three of them went to their rooms, too tired to eat. On her bed Suki found the old recorder and microphone, and remembered Levi. She hadn't thought of him all day! What sort of a sister did that make her? Perhaps she should give the old cassette machine a try after all. Levi couldn't read anything she wrote to him but maybe he would be able to hear her voice; there was probably an old cassette player somewhere in the hospital at Redknife. Tomorrow there would be a plane, and the post from Whale Bay would be collected. So if she was going to do it, it had to be now.

It took her a few minutes to work out which buttons to press on the old machine. Then she cleared her throat and began, in English:

"I'm sorry that you're sick..."

No, that wasn't right.

"I hope you'll be feeling..."

It all sounded wrong somehow. What *could* she say? *Please don't die!* Saying she was sorry and pleading with him to live would do no good. What Levi needed to hear was something new, something outside of the old life they'd both lived back in Ullavit. The life that had led her to be in trouble at school and him to be lying in a hospital bed.

The little red "record" light winked at her as she began again, in Inuktitut this time. She told her brother about the sigh of the sled and the patter of the dogs' feet; the tongues of snow pointing the way home. But most of all, she told him about *arviq*.

"It was right beside us, Levi, and so big it was as if an island had come to life and swum under the boat. When it breathed I felt the deep breath in my own chest, like singing... You have to come here, so you can go out on the ocean and see the whales. Maybe you could hunt them, like our ancestor, so all of Whale Bay could have maktak* *to eat for a year!"*

---

*maktak the skin of bowhead whales – a valued food for Inuit.

She imagined her voice in the quiet hospital room; her words tracing a meaning in Levi's sleeping mind, like the scratched lines of scrimshaw making a picture on the pale, blank face of a bone.

In the morning, as she put the tape in an envelope to post to the hospital in Redknife, the news came through on the radio: Levi Kaluak was still critically ill and in a coma, but the minister's son, Peter Oolik, had died in the night.

Chapter Eight

The sun had begun staying up all night, leaving the horizon behind for twenty-four hours of every day. All day and all through the light night, birds called. Plants grew so fast that Suki felt flowers just waited for her back to be turned, then sprang up in moments. The dogs grew scruffy, moulting their thick winter coats, and the snow buntings* stole the wisps of fur for their nests.

The snow and ice around the house melted, until there were just small patches left in the shadiest spots. The ice in the bay creaked and grumbled, as if talking about how painful it was to melt and break. A fat blue finger of clear water grew down the bay, getting closer and closer until it touched the rocks below the houses. A big plane came from Redknife with a mini digger, and the Red Hand men began making the foundations of the new dock.

Time went on. Weeks passed. But still Levi did not wake.

*snow bunting a small sparrow-sized Arctic bird.

Since the narwhal trip, Jaiku had been limping too much to walk to Whale Bay, so on Sunday nights, Eli came with his truck to pick the three of them up to come for a visit, and so that Suki could speak to her mum on Eli's phone. Sarah had got a job in Redknife, so she could stay and visit the hospital every day. Sarah said Peter's father, Minister Joseph Oolik, visited too, every week.

"I think it helps him to worry about Levi," Sarah said. "He likes your tapes, Suki – he always says so. We look forward to them."

Minister Oolik sent a new recording device, with a better microphone, so Suki could put her recordings on a tiny memory card and post it every week. The recordings became a weekly diary of her life in Whale Bay. How Noah had shot a caribou up in the hills, and how Jaiku had showed Suki the way to turn the skin into leather and then cut it with an *ulu**. How the Red Hand Oil men talked about what a busy port Whale Bay would be one day, and how the elders grumbled about it. How she'd learned to

*ulu a woman's semi-circular knife.

hunt ducks, catch fish, paddle a kayak and cook bannock. Suki felt Jaiku and Noah had taught her more than any teacher but it was sad that so many of the other inhabitants of Whale Bay seemed almost as asleep as her brother.

Her mum told her all the time that people came out of comas after months, years sometimes; eight weeks was nothing. But as the summer went on, and Levi showed no sign of improvement, Suki began to doubt that her recordings were helping him at all. So, one week when she'd forgotten to post the card it didn't seem to matter. But on the following Sunday night, Sarah sounded excited when she spoke on the phone.

"Your recording didn't make it this week, Suki," she began, "so I replayed that first one – the one about the whales. And when it came to the whale part, *Levi squeezed my hand*."

Suki felt her heart leap.

"Are you sure?"

"Sure as sure. I stopped the tape and played

that bit again, and he *definitely* squeezed my hand. *Twice!*"

"Oh, Mum!"

"They're going to do another test. Some brain scan or something. I'll call you at Eli's on Wednesday night."

"Thanks, Mum! Are you OK?"

"Yes, Suki. I'm OK. You?"

Suki nodded her head, even though her mum couldn't see her. "Yeah, I love it here, except I miss Levi and..." she added, "I miss you."

Her mum went very quiet on the other end of the phone.

"I miss you too," she answered at last. "And when this is all over, I'll be a better mum to you, Suki. I promise."

Suki's mind was racing. She walked outside to find Jaiku, who was sitting with Eli and Noah on the porch, like three figures on a mantlepiece. Jaiku was darning some of Eli's socks, while Noah and Eli shared a beer and talked about long ago. Suki told them the good news that Levi had begun to wake up, and that it was hearing about *arviq* that had done it. Then she took a deep breath and told them her idea:

"We have to go and find bowheads, get really close to them. If I could tell Levi about *that,* I'm sure he'd get better!"

Noah stared at her and Eli spluttered on his beer. "Nobody knows where to look for *arviq* now the bowhead hunters are all dead," he exclaimed.

Noah agreed. "It was just luck that we saw the one we did. They'll be far out at the mouth of the bay and it takes a day to get out there by boat, and then we'd have to search..."

"That's a lot of fuel," added Eli. "We might be out at sea searching for days..."

"*And* we'd need a second boat to carry supplies. Which we don't have," Noah said.

"We can't just go chasing bowheads," Eli shook his head sadly. "Things aren't the way they were in the old days!"

Suki looked from one old man to the other and felt a hot bubble of anger boil up so fast the words were out of her mouth before she had time to stop them.

"That's all you ever think about," she cried. "The old days. Everybody in Whale Bay just goes on and on about the past. What about *now*? What about the *future*? What good is it to Levi to hear how things used to be? How is *that* going to help him live?"

Suki turned and ran. Her anger carried her all the way back to Jaiku's house. She went into her room, shut the door and played the loudest music she could find through her headphones. Eli's old truck drew up without her hearing and it was only when Jaiku came and sat on her bed that Suki even opened her eyes. She took out her headphones and sat up. Suki knew it was time to say sorry for having been so disrespectful, but to her surprise it was Jaiku who was apologizing.

"I'm sorry, Suki," she said. "You are right. It's no help to anyone looking backwards the way we do. Come!" Jaiku took Suki's hand and led her into the kitchen, where Noah and Eli were sitting at the table, looking rather like two small boys who had been told off. Jaiku stood at the end of the table with her arms folded and her lips pressed together in a line. For a moment no one said anything, then Noah cleared his throat and said, "It is true we don't know how to *hunt arviq*," he said, "but we could *visit* him."

"We must find the fuel and the boat," said Eli.

"Yes," Noah concluded. "We have a young man's spirit to hunt!"

Jaiku nodded and smiled. "I'll make some cocoa," she said. "We have planning to do."

News of the planned "whale visiting" spread through the village like electricity. Everyone already knew about Jaiku's great-grandson being in hospital. They knew, too, why he was there; many families had lost young people in the same way; young men and women who had no hope and felt too sad to want to go on living. But when they heard that

Levi might be called out of his coma by his sister and a *whale*, for the first time in years they had something new to talk about. All through Monday people dropped by with contributions, from tents to caribou jerky, or just to wish them well. Jaiku didn't stop smiling all day.

"I haven't seen Whale Bay so alive since I was a child," she said. "It's like everyone's woken up!"

Cans of fuel, too, appeared outside Jaiku's house.

"We've got enough fuel to get halfway to Greenland and back," said Noah, "but we still need another boat."

"Lucy's brother's got a good-sized boat," said Jaiku. "I'll ask him."

On Tuesday morning, while Jaiku was out seeing Lucy's brother, and Suki was helping Noah put fish into the smoker, Eli drew up in his rusty truck.

"You won't believe what I've got to tell you!" he said. "The oil guys want to help out with their big boat!"

"They'll have to drive it a bit quieter than normal if we're looking for *arviq*!" exclaimed Noah.

"I already told them that," Eli chuckled.

Suki grinned at the two elders. "How soon can we go?" she said.

Noah and Eli laughed. "The weather's set fair," Eli said. "Tomorrow?"

Noah nodded. "Tomorrow."

It would mean that Suki would not be back to get the news about Levi's brain tests but when she did get back she'd have the best medicine ready to deliver!

Almost everyone in Whale Bay came to wave them off. People that Suki had never seen in all her weeks at Jaiku's appeared on the jetty. Pete Laplaque's grandmother, Illisapi, was carried down in her easy chair. Nobody knew exactly how many birthdays she'd had, but Eli said it was at least a hundred. She had a faint whispery voice, like paper.

"I want to see Manattiaq's girl," she breathed, "Jaiku's grandchild. Where is she?"

Her milky eyes searched without seeing, so Suki came and took her hand. "I'm here!" she said gently.

"This is a great day!" the ancient lady whispered. "The whole community together, wanting the same thing. This is the start of something good!"

Noah put a hand on Suki's shoulder. "Time to go," he said.

"Goodbye, Illisapi!" Suki said.

"Hunt well, Little Whale Warrior!" whispered the old lady. "You are hunting for our future!"

Chapter Nine

Zac's boat floated beside the shiny Red Hand boat. Pete Laplaque, his brother Stephan, David's grown-up son Martin, grumpy Joe and most of the stores and camping gear went in the Red Hand boat with the two oil guys, Brad and Bryan. Suki got into Zac's boat with Zac, David, Eli and Noah. She was the only young person and the only girl; just like the scrimshaw picture of Manattiaq's whale crew. The boats drew away from the jetty and the whole village waved and kept waving until they had shrunk to coloured dots in the distance.

Suki sat in the bow, with the deep blue of the ocean filling her eyes, and Minister Oolik's machine on her lap, ready to record every detail of the trip for Levi. All around the Arctic summer popped with life. Ducks and seabirds splintered the surface of the water into splashes of light, or criss-crossed the bright air with their calls. The boats made their way slowly along the western edge of Funk Island, which stood in the middle of the bay. Zac steered under the tall cliffs so they could look up at the high-rise city of seabirds, thousands of murres* and fulmars* stacked on the rocky ledges. They stopped the engine and drifted for a time while Suki recorded all the sounds for Levi, and Brad and Bryan took pictures.

"Used to come out here when I was a boy and catch murres. Tasty they are!" said Eli.

"I never liked 'em much. Too much bone, not enough meat," Noah said.

"We better quit birdwatching or we won't see any whales for Levi!" said David.

On they went, slowly and steadily, Zac's outboard puttering and the Red Hand boat purring. The island fell away behind them and in the distance the narrow entrance to the bay could be seen. White icebergs dotted the darker blue of the open ocean beyond.

"Why don't the bergs wash into the bay, Uncle Noah?" Suki asked.

*murre Canadian/US word for a guillemot – a pigeon-sized black and white seabird.
*fulmar a large seagull-like bird, related to the albatross.

"There's a kind of lip of shallower water at the entrance, keeps 'em out. Just one deep channel in the middle," Noah answered.

"Then deeper water on this side," Eli added. "My grandpa used to say that's the place *arviq* like best!"

"Why on earth didn't you say that before?" Noah scolded.

It took another hour to get close to the mouth of the bay. The wind there was stronger and the waves bigger. The two boats danced about. Suki was determined not to be seasick, but even fresh bannock didn't make her feel hungry. For another three hours they went back and forth across the bay, scanning the water all around, and saw nothing but choppy blue sea and sky.

"We should head in and make camp," Noah said. "Get some rest."

They brought the boats ashore on a shingle beach on the south side of Hand Island, a tiny scrap of land on the east side of the bay. They pitched tents, made a driftwood fire and sat talking quietly while Brad and Bryan roasted chicken and handed out potato chips.

"Could we hunt bowheads again one day?" Suki heard Martin ask his father.

David sighed and shook his head. "We'd have to find some first!"

"You don't think our chances are good?" Martin asked, but David was silent. Suki lay in her tent thinking about that silence. What if, after all this, they didn't find whales? What if she brought back no spirit for Levi and no hope for Whale Bay? Would everyone sit on their couches talking about the past until they died?

A gunshot woke her. She was outside her tent in three seconds. The wobbling white bottom of a polar bear was running out of camp! Zac fired a second shot over its head. It looked over its shoulder and ran on. "Must have swum out from the mainland," he said.

"Smelt that store-bought chicken, I expect," David said in English to Brad, who poked his sleepy head from their tent.

"We might as well get going," said Zac. "Looks like everyone's awake anyway."

They were back on the water by 4 a.m., but there were clouds gathering. The sea grew choppy; spotting a whale blow was going to be difficult among the hills and valleys of waves and swells. No one said it, but the wind was rising and the prospect of returning to Whale Bay without having seen a single whale was growing with every gust.

Then, right at the mouth of the bay, Suki saw a black triangle slicing through the waves. She'd seen those kind of fins on TV, and knew that they belonged to killer whales, orcas, but did they live here? Suki blinked and looked again. Two more triangles had joined the first, then black-and-white snouts poked out and she could see faint puffs of breath. Now she was certain.

"Orcas!" she sang out. "There!"

"You have good whale eyes, Suki," David was smiling.

"Manattiaq's girl for sure!" added Zac, with a grin.

Now Suki spotted something more: between their boat and the orcas, there was a line of blows, much, much bigger than the orcas'.

"Bowhead!" Suki cried. "And they're heading this way."

"The orcas must be chasing them!" said Noah.

"I saw an orca take a narwhal calf one time," said Eli. "When I was out catching murres."

"But the bowheads are so much bigger!" exclaimed Suki.

"Orcas are smart," said Eli. "And they hunt in a pack like wolves."

It was hard to tell how many bowheads there were altogether as they didn't all blow at the same time.

"Six?" Zac suggested.

"More!" Noah said.

"Could be ten maybe?" Eli suggested.

One thing was clear: one of the whales was trailing, and beside it was a tiny calf. That was what the orcas were after!

"The orcas are closing in," exclaimed Suki. "We've got to do something!"

Eli and Noah looked at each other. "They're just hunting," said Eli.

"We shouldn't butt into their business," Noah agreed.

Suki looked at David and Zac, who didn't seem as certain as the two elders.

"We Inuit, we don't take narwhal with calves," said David.

"Yes," said Zac, "we wouldn't be asking the orcas to do something we wouldn't do."

Suki held her breath. The dark fins of the orcas were well inside the bay now. Eli and Noah exchanged glances; everyone else seemed to be waiting.

"Well..." said Eli slowly, "I guess we *could* put

the boats between the orcas and the mum and her calf..."

Zac smiled, and wheeled the boat round. David spoke to the oil guys' boat on the walkie-talkie and, like the two fingers of a pinch, the boats curved round, to get between the approaching orcas and the mother and her calf. For a few minutes the orcas kept coming, and then their fins disappeared. The whale and her calf had slowed to a stop, their backs grey at the surface, the calf's blows close together, betraying its fear and tiredness. Suki held her breath, expecting that the orcas had dived under them and would pop up right next to their prey. Minutes passed. Everyone scanned the choppy sea.

Then the tall black fins of the orcas reappeared – heading out to sea. The mother and calf were safe! Even Noah and Eli were smiling. Brad and Bryan gave each other high fives.

Slowly, the bowheads began to move, following the path the others had taken.

"We need to head back. The wind's getting up,"

said Zac. "But we can keep behind the whales –
they're going our way!"

Keeping the bowhead blows in sight, the two
boats came round to the southern side of Funk
Island and in the calmer water out of the wind
found more whales. A *lot* more whales!

Suki gazed around at the blows, like a forest of
breath growing from the rough blue of the sea. One
after another the whales dived, lifting their huge

tail flukes clear of the surface in slow motion, and then slipping out of sight.

"Twenty-two blows I counted!" exclaimed David. "Make that twenty-three!"

"And there's more over there!" said Zac.

"There are calves!" Suki said. "I've seen at least four!"

Noah and Eli patted each other on the back. Noah seemed close to tears. "This is what we came

for" he said. "Levi's spirit is here. The spirits of all our ancestors with him!"

Carefully, they edged the boats amongst the whales so Suki could get close enough to record the sound of a blow over the noise of the waves and wind. Then a whale swam under their boat and surfaced within metres of their bow.

"I think I've got it, Uncle Noah!" Suki cried and felt her face shining with delight, her heart singing against her ribs.

"It's true what Uncle Noah said," she whispered into the machine to Levi, "when a whale passes underneath your boat, you *do* understand your place in the world."

Suki tucked the machine and all its precious recording out of reach of sea and rain.

"Time to go!" said Zac. "Bad weather coming in."

They turned around and fled from the waves and wind, back up the bay, running from the storm as the *arviq* had run from the orcas. The journey home was a battle and all the way Suki willed them to go faster. She wanted the medicine she had for Levi to get to him as soon as possible.

They arrived back in flurries of snow but in spite of the weather the village had turned out to welcome them and hear about the whales. Suki felt as triumphant as Manattiaq, hauling her mighty catch back to feed her people. She ran up the jetty to find Jaiku. But her great-granny was grim-faced.

"Joseph Oolik has bought you a ticket to Redknife," she said. "I'm sorry, Suki, but Levi is dying."

Chapter Ten

The brain scan had been hopeful, but now it was Levi's body, not his mind, that was giving out. A fever was consuming him, burning his life away.

All through the flight and the drive to the hospital Suki sat very still, a lump in her throat and a knot in her chest. She clutched the recorder so tightly her knuckles were numb and white. She concentrated hard to keep going until she got to Levi. Sarah was waiting at the hospital doors. One look told Suki that she too was holding tight inside. They barely spoke. They didn't need to.

Levi was hardly a person. Just a thing made of flesh with tubes coming out of him. But Suki willed herself not to cry. All that mattered was that he should hear her recording. Someone brought a little speaker and put it on his bedside table. Suki plugged in the device, and pressed play. She took her brother's hand, too hot, too thin and too limp, and shut her eyes.

The whole trip was there. From Illisapi's papery blessing and the cheering of the crowd on the jetty, through the crackling campfire and the shouts of surprise as the bear ran off, to the orca attack and the exclamations from the crew. Suki's hand felt for the slightest flicker, the smallest hint of life from Levi's burning skin. But there was nothing, nothing, nothing.

An icy thread of despair began to snake into her heart.

And then…

Huuuwwufff.

The microphone had picked up the bowhead's blow beautifully. It sounded even louder than it had from the boat, and so close! It was a deep, echoing rasp, as if air was rushing from a huge cave; a sound imprinted with vastness and dignity.

Levi's grip was so sudden and so strong that Suki cried out. It felt almost like a dying spasm. But when her voice on the recording whispered, *"It's true what Uncle Noah said, when a whale passes underneath your boat, you do understand your place in the world"*, Levi squeezed her hand again, and kept squeezing. She caught hold of his other hand, in spite of the tangle of tubes, and she gripped that too. It felt as if she was lifting his whole weight, hauling him up with all her strength. Her body shook with the effort and she felt her mother's arms go around her. They pulled together with all their might and Levi opened his eyes.

Epilogue

Graceful as a dancer, Suki stood in the bow of the *Zodiac* with the fine harpoon raised high above her head, ready. With great care Levi steered the boat closer to the v-shaped head in the water. At just the right moment, he dropped their speed to nothing and the whale moved ahead a little. Suki's body, taut as a spring, loosed the harpoon. Its sharp point pierced the whale's flesh and quick as a flash Suki pulled it back, releasing the small electronic tag into the whale's skin. It would track the whale and tell them where she went and how deep she dove.

A little spooked by the unexpected pinprick, the big female dived with her calf beside her.

"Good job, little sister!" Levi said.

"Good driving, big brother!" said Suki.

Levi stopped the engine and turned to the figure hunched over a laptop in the bottom of the boat.

"Got a signal, Outi?" he said in English; like

many of the scientists from other countries who visited the Peter Oolik Research Station, the young Greenlander didn't speak Inuktitut.

"Yep! There it is," she said, pointing to the little blip on the screen.

The three young people smiled at each other.

"That's five females with calves tagged!" said Suki. "Now we can find out *exactly* where they go when they leave the Sanctuary."

The Sanctuary was what they all called Whale Bay now, because that's what it was, a sanctuary for bowhead whales, safe from hunting, from the traffic of oil tankers and from orcas who didn't really like coming up the bay. It had been Joseph Oolik's idea and he'd even managed to get Red Hand Oil to donate some money to pay for the research centre in exchange for finding another place to put their dock, on a more populated bit of coastline. Not everyone in Whale Bay had liked the idea at first. After all, if *arviq* had come back, people said, doesn't that mean we can go back to hunting bowheads, like we used to? That's what Suki had thought too, until Levi talked her round.

"The whales saved my life," he said. "I have a debt to pay them. Besides," he'd added, "if we protect the calves, then there'll be *arviq* for Inuit to see far into the future."

When Minister Oolik announced there would be jobs for people in the new research centre *and* they'd need the elders to help run the Traditional Skills courses for Inuit youngsters, most people stopped grumbling about not being allowed to hunt bowheads.

"All that's the past, anyway," Jaiku said. "It's the future we should be thinking about now!"

"And in the future," Noah said, with a gleam in his eye, "I will have to keep at least five dog teams so I can teach more youngsters the best form of transport in the world!"

Today, the sea was so glassy calm that the only breaks in the reflection of the sky were the last remaining flecks of sea ice. Suki pulled the little scrap of skin from the end of the harpoon. Back in the lab the skin would help them work out which of the other bowheads this whale was related to, and if she had experienced pollution in her long life. Suki dropped the skin scrap into a test tube and wrote on the label.

"Everything is so much easier when it's calm like this!" she said.

"I'd be bored if it was like this all the time," said Levi. "I like battling big waves!"

"You two should come to Greenland in the spring," said Outi. "I need your expert help to tag the male bowheads. Who knows, we may find they come here and sing under *your* ice in the winter!"

"That would be great," said Levi. "Hey, maybe I could do my Masters in Greenland."

"I could teach you to drive a dog team," Suki said to Outi.

"Everything's possible!" said Levi. "Everything!"

Levi started up the engine. There were so many plans. So much future to live for. They turned the boat up the blue finger of the bay and headed back to shore.

LIVING WITH WHALES

"There are many wonderful animals, but whales are best of all."

This is what an Inuk hunter said about bowhead whales, the biggest species of whale to share the Inuit's Arctic environment. If you saw a bowhead from a boat, as Suki does in this story, you would recognize it instantly. You would see the V-shaped blow, billowing up six metres into the cold air. You would see the broad, smooth back, with no dorsal fin. You might well see the white chin, as bowhead whales like to swim on their backs, and the great curve of the jaw. You'd certainly notice the size, as an average bowhead is around seventeen metres (fifty-six feet) long and weighs eighty tonnes! Your bowhead would be moving slowly through the water compared with other kinds of whale, swimming close to the surface or sometimes diving to depths of thirty metres to find food: huge clouds of small, shrimp-like creatures that bowheads sift from the sea with the interlocking bristles of the hundreds

of four-metre-long baleen plates that fill their mouths.

Bowhead whales are never far from sea ice, and they are well equipped for the freezing temperatures. A thick layer of blubber keeps out the cold, and their huge heads can act as ice breakers if needed, smashing through ice up to thirty centimetres thick to find air to breathe and to make a route through the frozen sea. In the winter they swim a little further south, to places just outside the Arctic Circle. In the summer they follow the shrinking ice north, high into the "land of the midnight sun", where for six months of the year the sea bursts with life.

Their size, their blubber and their long baleen plates made bowheads the perfect prey for human hunters. But it took courage, ingenuity and cooperation to kill such a huge creature at sea, bring it to shore and cut up its body, using weapons and tools made from only bone and stone. For hundreds of years Inuit and other native peoples, from Alaska to Greenland and Northern Siberia, hunted bowheads. Every part of the whale was used: the meat and vitamin-rich skin, or *maktak*, were important foods, and the blubber provided oil for lamps. A single bowhead could feed a whole village. Not surprisingly, the bowhead became the centre of Arctic culture, the heart of beliefs and stories — and whaling captains were very important community leaders.

But the very things that made the bowhead useful for Arctic peoples also made them a perfect target for whaling ships from the UK, Europe and the USA. From the seventeenth century, bowhead hunting spread across the Arctic from Spitsbergen, Norway, reaching what is now Arctic Canada in the eighteenth century. But these whalers weren't killing a few whales to feed their communities. Hundreds of thousands of bowhead whales were killed to light homes all over Europe and America and to provide whale bone, a bendy and durable material that was used to do many of the same jobs that plastics do today.

So many bowhead whales were killed that by the late nineteenth century there were almost none left for the Inuit in Canada and Greenland, who had to hunt smaller creatures. Hunting no longer involved

THE FACT IS

107

the whole community, and Inuit culture changed as a result. Settlements broke up into smaller family bands that moved with the seasons to find food and shelter.

Today bowhead whales, like many other species of whale, are protected by law. Big whaling ships are forbidden to kill whales, and bowhead populations in some parts of the Arctic are beginning to recover. Inuit communities have the right to kill small numbers of bowheads, and a very few communities now hunt bowheads to provide food for themselves and maintain their traditional way of life. Some people argue that no one, not even Inuit, should be allowed to kill bowheads; but many scientists agree that the small number killed by native people do not, for now, put the species in danger. However, bowheads do face new threats today: drilling for oil and increased shipping traffic put them at risk from pollution, disturbance and injury through collisions; climate change may reduce the amount of food for them and possibly even entirely destroy the sea ice to which they are adapted.

Climate change has a more drastic impact on the

Arctic than any other place on earth. Areas that were once under thick sea ice and inaccessible are now open sea, so what used to be a frozen wilderness could become shipping highways and oil fields. This is going to have a significant effect on Arctic wildlife like bowhead whales. Their future is far from certain.

Many Inuit, too, feel threatened by the modern world. Without their traditional hunting lifestyle, some communities struggle with unemployment and social problems. Young people are especially badly affected, and sometimes turn to drugs, alcohol or even suicide as a way out.

But there is hope. Some Inuit are becoming champions of the Arctic environment, speaking up for the land and the animals that were traditionally at the centre of their lives. One community, Clyde River on the north coast of Baffin Island in Northern Canada, has worked with the government and the World Wide Fund for Nature (WWF) to set up three wildlife reserves in the region. One of these is Isabella Bay, where once big whaling ships came to kill bowheads. Now, the hundreds of bowheads that gather there in late summer, to feed and take refuge from killer whales, are protected. No hunting, oil drilling or other activity that might threaten the whales is allowed. The reserves are also intended to give young Inuit the chance to train as wildlife biologists, conservationists, tour guides and educators, and to become the stewards of the wild Arctic in the future. The WWF is also working with scientists, businesses and communities to try to ensure that the problems that

This bowhead in Greenland is about to be tagged using a harpoon-thrown lance

animals face aren't added to by pollution, disturbance and over-hunting or over-fishing. Perhaps the world can one day learn to love and respect the Arctic just as the Inuit always have.

Look out for these other HEROES OF THE WILD stories

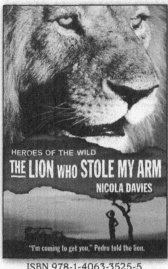

ISBN 978-1-4063-3525-5

ISBN 978-1-4063-4087-7

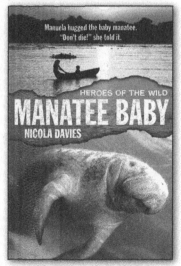

ISBN 978-1-4063-4088-4

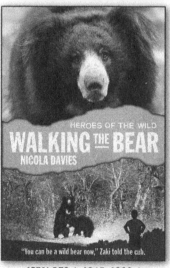

ISBN 978-1-4063-4089-1